AF583753

A WOOLLY TALE

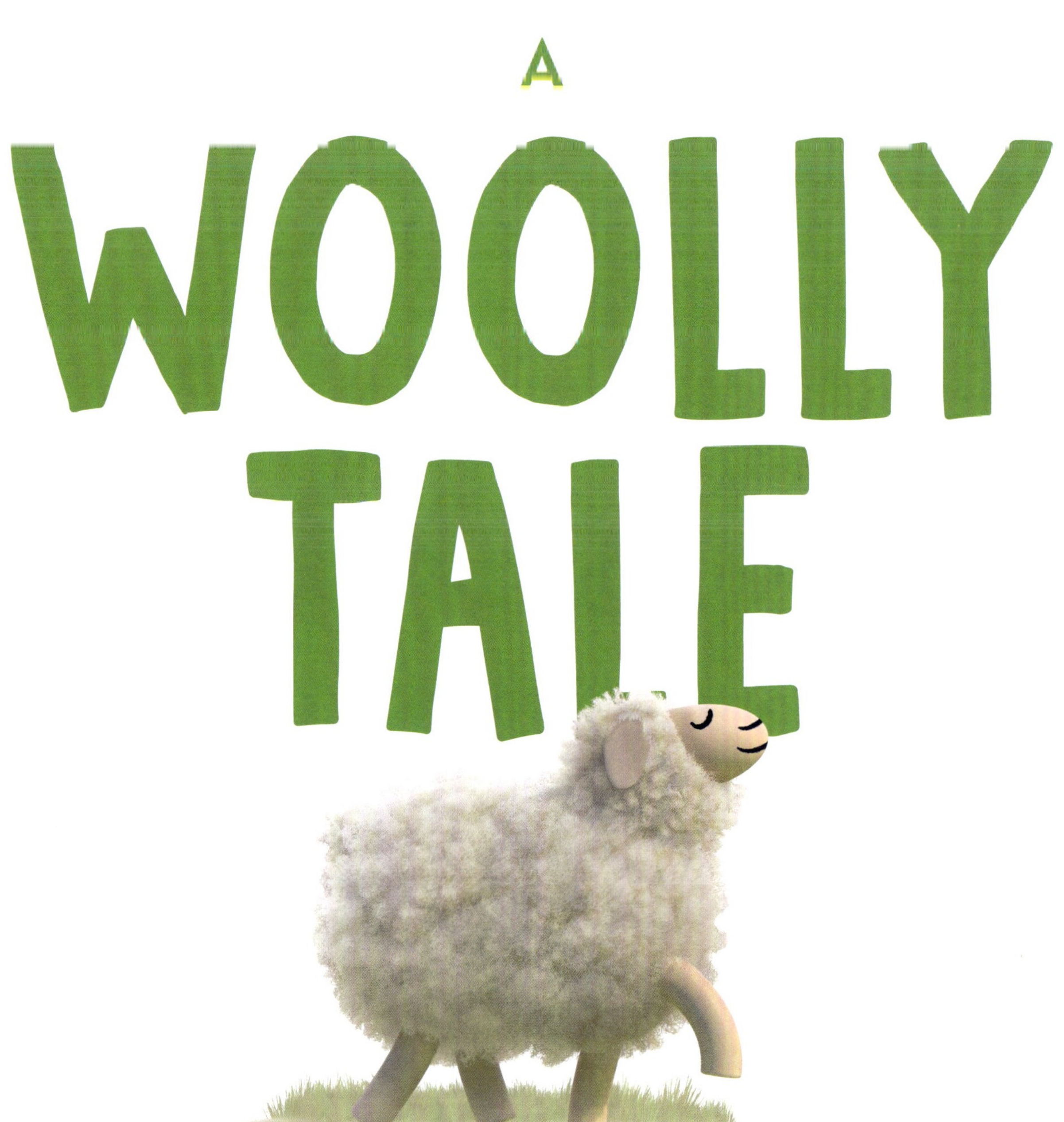

by **Jackie Hosking**

illustrated by **Paul Lalo**

national museum australia

Chris the sheep lived on a farm with all of his brothers and sisters.

Like the rest of the flock, Chris was a merino sheep, and merino sheep are bred for their soft fine wool.

Every year the sheep are taken to the shed to be shorn.

This year was the first time
for Chris and he was very nervous.

'I don't want to be shorn,' he said.
'What if the clippers nick my skin?'

'Don't be such a lamb,' said his brothers and sisters. 'If you don't get shorn ...'

'Yes?' said Chris.

But none of the other sheep knew what
would happen if he didn't get shorn.

On shearing day, Chris went for a walk to calm himself down.

All sorts of thoughts buzzed around his head.

Chris became more and more worried. Then he saw his chance – there was a hole in the fence!

He squeezed himself through and disappeared into the bush beyond.

After some time he came upon a stream.

When he lowered his head to sip the cool, refreshing water, Chris saw his reflection. What a sad, sorry sight he looked.

No one will want wool from this scrawny looking sheep, he thought. I should stay away until my wool is thicker. Then no one will make fun of me and the shearer will be less likely to nick my skin.

Merinos are very good at foraging for food and enjoy eating all sorts of plants, so Chris had no trouble finding things to eat.

He spent his days admiring the wildflowers, talking to the parrots and following the stream up into the mountains.

The seasons came and went.

In spring he frolicked with the butterflies.

In summer he kept cool in the stream.

In autumn he enjoyed the milder days.

And in winter – well, each winter he felt terrific.

Years passed, and Chris's wool grew and grew.

Then one day he came across a very wild and wiry looking dingo.

'Whatever are you?' asked the dingo, licking his lips. 'I've not seen anything like you in the bush before.'

'I'm Chris,' said Chris.
'I'm a merino sheep.'

'A sheep?' said the dingo. 'I've heard of sheep,' and drool dribbled from his hungry mouth.

'You're a very tasty – I mean, healthy looking sheep,' said the dingo.

‘Thank you,’ said Chris. ‘I’ve been living my best life! Although lately I’m not moving as well as I used to.’

‘Perhaps now it’s time for me to return to the farm.’

'Hold up there, Chris,' the dingo said, not wanting to let his dinner slip away.

'Wouldn't you fancy a snack before you go? I've got tasty treats just a short stroll away! You'll certainly need the energy for your long journey home.'

'How very kind of you,' said Chris, and he followed the dingo, moving slowly under his big woolly coat.

But before they arrived, the dingo turned and pounced on Chris.

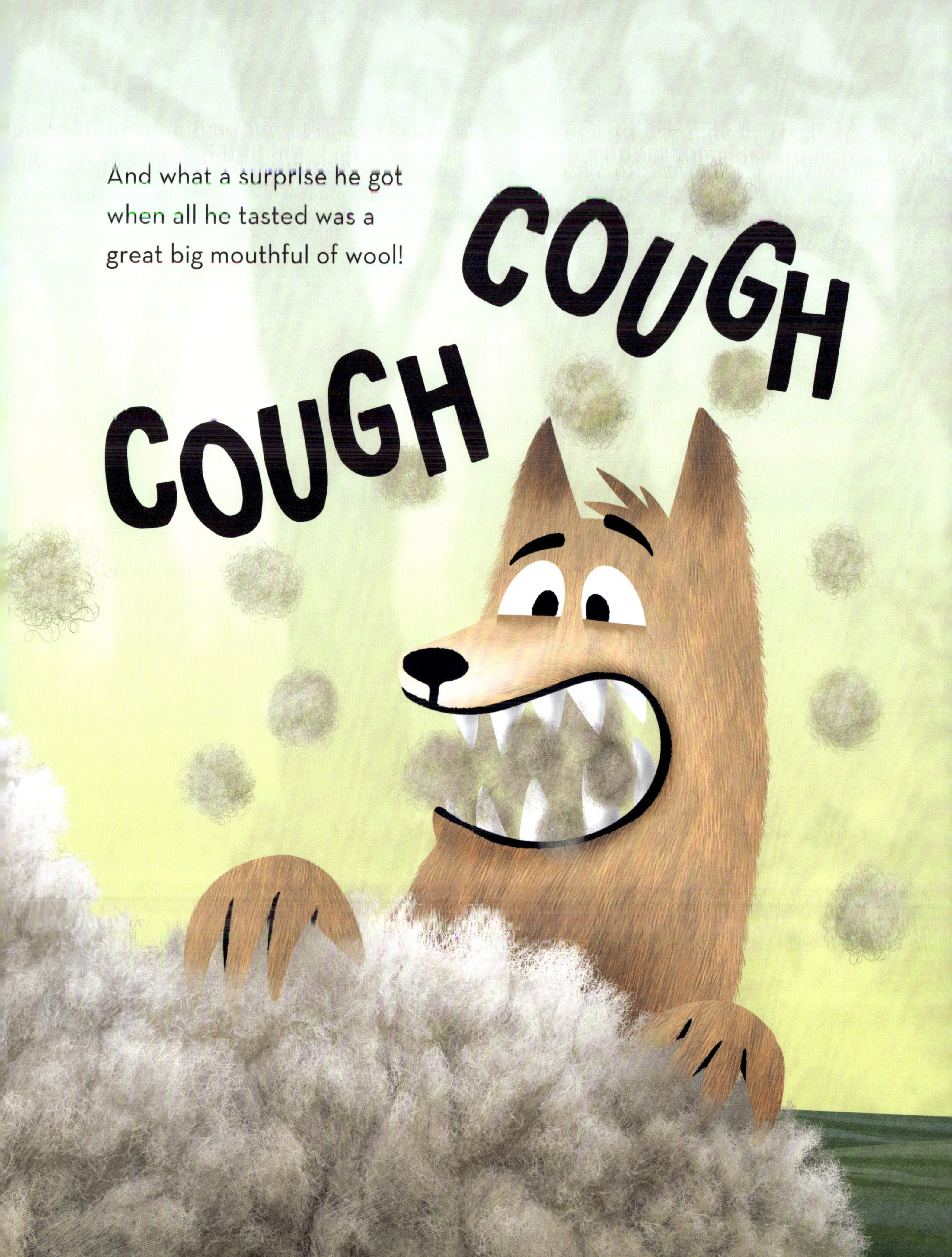
And what a surprise he got when all he tasted was a great big mouthful of wool!
COUGH
COUGH

Chris was also surprised.
'Whatever are you doing?' he asked.

But the dingo just kept on leaping and snapping and snarling until eventually he gave up.

'You're not a sheep,' he whined. 'You're nothing but a great big ball of wool.'

'I am?' said Chris, thrilled to bits.

And with that he shuffled and tripped his way back to the farm ...

... where he discovered that he was, in fact, the biggest ball of wool in the world.

After he was very carefully shorn by one of the world's best shearers, Chris felt amazing! Lighter, cooler, happier.

'What a fine, brave sheep you are,' said the shearer. And Chris, the woolliest sheep in the world, agreed.

For all my fellow adventurers, Thomas, Ollie, Sammy, Alice, Morgan, Alaska, Fintan, Tiernan, Evie and Zoe, here's to living your best lives.

— Jackie Hosking

The story

Jackie Hosking is a Nigerian-born Cornish Australian poet and picture book author who loves to tell a funny story. She wrote *A Woolly Tale* based on a true story about Chris the sheep, who wandered into the bush near Canberra and got lost for nearly five years. When he was finally found, his wool set a record for the world's heaviest fleece – now on display at the National Museum of Australia. This playful fictional tale imagines what Chris might have been up to during his adventure in the bush.

The series

A Woolly Tale is the third in a series of five picture books featuring Australian stories inspired by the National Museum of Australia's immersive play space for children, the Tim and Gina Fairfax Discovery Centre.

Other titles in the series include *The Bunyip and the Stars* by Adam Duncan and *How Mother Kangaroo Got Her Pouch* by Rebecca Beetson and are available from the Museum Shop shop.nma.gov.au.

Published by the National Museum of Australia Press on the lands of the Ngunnawal and Ngambri Kamberri. Printed in Australia on the lands of the Wathaurong.

Editor: Minnie Doron
Designer: Anna McGregor
Illustrator: Paul Lalo, Soymilk Studio
Illustration concept designer: Jenni Vigaud
Printer: Adams Print
Typeset in Neutraface and Jealous Punk

A catalogue record for this book is available from the National Library of Australia.

978-1-921953-47-7

First published in 2024

National Museum of Australia Press
Lawson Crescent, Acton,
Canberra ACT 2601
Australia

publications@nma.gov.au